**Welcome to ALADDIN QUIX!**

If you are looking for fast, fun-to-read stories with colorful characters, lots of kid-friendly humor, easy-to-follow action, entertaining story lines, and lively illustrations, then **ALADDIN QUIX** is for you!

But wait, there's more!

If you're also looking for stories with tables of contents; word lists; about-the-book questions; 64, 80, or 96 pages; short chapters; short paragraphs; and large fonts, then **ALADDIN QUIX** is *definitely* for you!

**ALADDIN QUIX:** The next step between ready to reads and longer, more challenging chapter books, for readers five to eight years old.

ROBERT QUACKENBUSH

ALADDIN QUIX

New York London Toronto Sydney New Delhi

ALADDIN QUIX
Simon & Schuster Children's Publishing Division
1230 Avenue of the Americas, New York, New York 10020
This Aladdin QUIX paperback edition January 2019

Also available in an Aladdin QUIX hardcover edition.

Designed by Tiara Iandiorio
The illustrations for this book were rendered in pen and ink and wash.
The text of this book was set in Archer Medium.
Manufactured in the United States of America 1218 OFF
2 4 6 8 10 9 7 5 3 1
Library of Congress Control Number 2018959529
ISBN 978-1-5344-1398-6 (hc)
ISBN 978-1-5344-1397-9 (pbk)
ISBN 978-1-5344-1399-3 (eBook)

For Piet and Margie,

and now for Emma and Aidan

# Cast of Characters

**Miss Mallard:** World-famous ducktective

**innkeeper:** Runs the gloomy inn

**Julia Pintail:** Secret agent who meets Miss Mallard at the inn

**henchducks:** Smugglers who are looking for secret agent Julia Pintail

**farmer:** Person who owns the farm where Miss Mallard seeks refuge

**policeducks:** Officers who arrest the smugglers

# What's in Miss Mallard's Bag?

Miss Mallard has many detective tools she brings with her on her adventures around the world.

In her knitting bag she usually has:

- Newspaper clippings
- Knitting needles and yarn
- A magnifying glass
- A flashlight
- A mirror
- A travel guide
- Chocolates for her nephew

# Contents

# Gloomy Inn

While on a bicycle tour of Holland, **Miss Mallard**—the world-famous ducktective—took a wrong turn. She became separated from the other cyclists.

When she got back on the right

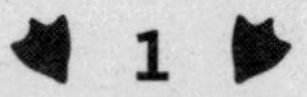

road, the tour group was nowhere in sight.

All day Miss Mallard pedaled hard and fast to catch up, but she was still way behind. **And she was so tired and hungry!**

Finally she decided to look for a place where she could eat and spend the night. Soon she came to an inn.

Miss Mallard parked her bike in front and entered the inn. The inside was very **gloomy**, with dark woodwork and furniture.

Everything lacked color. Even the flower vases were empty.

"Oh well," thought Miss Mallard. "It will do for one night."

She signed her name in the guest book.

"I'll pay for the room now," Miss Mallard said to the **innkeeper**. "I'll be leaving quite early in the morning. I'm hoping to catch up with my tour."

"Your room is the first door to the left as you go upstairs," said the innkeeper as he handed her a key. "Supper is now being served in the dining room."

Miss Mallard went up to her room to unpack her knitting bag. Then she went to the dining room. There she met another guest at the inn, **Julia Pintail**, who invited Miss Mallard to sit at her table.

"I'm so glad to meet you, Miss Mallard," said Julia happily. **"Your name is known all over the world!"**

During supper the two of them chatted about their travels.

Miss Mallard told her about visiting the pyramids in Egypt and the canals in Venice. Miss Pintail had been down the Amazon River and to the top of Mount Everest.

But all the while Miss Mallard noticed that her dinner companion was very, very nervous.

Julia kept glancing at the dining room entrance. From time to time she took a small black book from her purse and scribbled a few words in it.

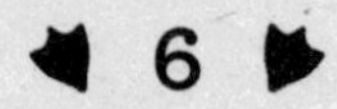

Suddenly, while having their dessert, **two tough-looking ducks** appeared at the dining room entrance. In a flash Julia ducked under the table.

"Pretend I'm not here," she whispered to Miss Mallard. "Tell me when those two ducks leave."

Miss Mallard waited. She saw the two ducks look around the room. Then they vanished.

"It's safe to come out now," said Miss Mallard to Julia.

Julia came out from under the

table and said, “Do you think they saw me?”

“I can’t be certain,” said Miss Mallard as she noticed the two ducks walking through the lobby. “What is this about?”

“I can tell you because I trust you,” said Julia. “But you must tell no one else. **I am a secret agent!** In a **quaint** bookshop in Amsterdam, I accidentally learned that a ring of **smugglers** has its headquarters in this area. They are smuggling stolen diamonds,

china, and old master paintings out of the country."

She paused and then said, "I'm positive that those two ducks are part of the ring. They have been following me everywhere. They are **henchducks**."

# 2

## Secret Code

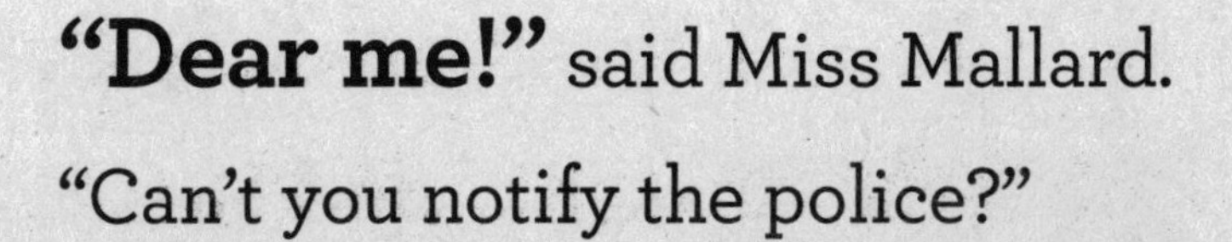

**"Dear me!"** said Miss Mallard. "Can't you notify the police?"

"After I find the **mastermind** of the operation," said Julia. "Then I plan to go to the police."

"Can I help?" asked Miss Mallard.

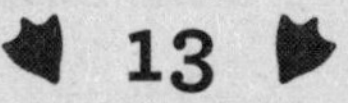

7
8
9
5
4
3

"In a way you are helping right now," said Julia. "I'll tell you about it in the morning. Please knock on my door when you are ready to leave. I'm in room three."

"Is six o'clock too early for you?" asked Miss Mallard.

"The earlier the better," replied Julia.

With that, they both said "good night" and went to their rooms.

**Promptly** at six the next morning, Miss Mallard knocked on Julia's door. There was no answer.

She knocked again. Still there was no answer. She turned the knob, the door opened, and she peeked inside. **Julia was gone and so were her things!**

Miss Mallard ran to the lobby to ask the innkeeper if he had seen Julia.

"Miss Pintail checked out late last night," said the innkeeper. "Two friends came for her."

*"Friends?"* asked Miss Mallard. "Were they wearing **trench coats** and dark glasses?"

"I don't know," answered the innkeeper. "I wasn't here at the time."

Miss Mallard shivered. She was sure Julia had been ducknapped. She raced from the lobby and hurried back to her room.

Once there, she reached for her knitting bag and felt around inside to see if she had packed everything. She felt something unfamiliar and pulled it out of the bag.

**"Julia's black book!"**

Miss Mallard gasped.

All at once, everything was clear to Miss Mallard. At supper, Julia had slipped the black book into Miss Mallard's knitting bag for safekeeping.

She must have planned to ask for it when Miss Mallard knocked on her door the next morning. But as she had just discovered, **Julia Pintail had been ducknapped!**

Miss Mallard thumbed through the black book. Julia's last entry was written in code:

"There's no time to **decode** this message," thought Miss Mallard. "I must go to the police at once. **There is not a moment to waste!"**

She went to the window to see if it was safe to leave. **The two henchducks were waiting outside!**

"Oh no," thought Miss Mallard. "The henchducks must have seen Julia and me together at dinner after all. I bet they figured out that she gave the black book to me. But what have they done with her? What will they do with me?"

EGDIRBO
REZEENST

# Dutch Disguise

Miss Mallard wondered how she could get past the henchducks. Luckily she remembered a Dutch costume, complete with wooden shoes, that she had bought during her travels.

She pulled it out of her knitting bag and quickly changed. Then she ran down the back stairs of the inn.

Outside, Miss Mallard saw a pail and a broom by the back door.

**"Aha!" she exclaimed.**

She put her knitting bag in the pail and took the pail and broom to the front of the inn. Then she began sweeping the front walk as though she worked at the inn. Fooled by her clever disguise, the henchducks ignored her.

As Miss Mallard swept, she kept edging closer to her bicycle, which was behind a tree. When she was close enough, she hopped onto it and took off.

But—**OOPS!**—it was hard to pedal in wooden shoes. They fell off her feet and hit the ground with a **clatter**. Snatching them up, Miss Mallard tossed them into her knitting bag and hurried on.

Miss Mallard pedaled with all her might across a field behind the inn. Then she saw a speeding

car racing along the road. One of the henchducks was inside!

**"Oh no!"** cried Miss Mallard aloud. "They saw me escape!"

There was no turning back. There was no going forward. A henchduck awaited her at each end of the field. She got off her bicycle and stood frozen in her tracks.

Just then a big tractor roared forward from a **cluster** of trees. It stopped in front of Miss Mallard.

"What are you doing in my

field?" demanded the **farmer** who was driving the tractor.

Before Miss Mallard could answer, he climbed down from his tractor, tossed Miss Mallard's bicycle on the back, and helped her **aboard**. Then he sped back to the group of trees.

"I'm sorry if I disturbed your field," said Miss Mallard. The farmer sneezed loudly.

"Here," said Miss Mallard. "Take one of my handkerchiefs.

**"Blasted cold!"** he said as

he set Miss Mallard's bicycle on the ground.

"Thank you!" Miss Mallard said. "I'll be on my way."

Miss Mallard got on her bicycle and pedaled quickly onto a path.

She knew that the henchducks would soon be after her, and she looked for a place to hide. The great ducktective raced along the path until she came to a bridge that led to a windmill.

**"This is the only place I can safely hide!"** she said.

She got off her bicycle and hauled it under the bridge.

Safely hidden, Miss Mallard took Julia's black book from her bag. She turned to the last entry and set to work decoding the message.

At first glance she couldn't make heads nor tails of the letters.

***"What does this mean?"***

she thought. But then she saw that the words were all written *backward*, with an *extra* letter added at the end of each word.

The decoded message said:

OVER THE BRIDGE

THE GOODS ARE STORED;

FIND THE SNEEZER,

HE MASTERMINDS THE **HOARD**!

# The Sneezer

**"Good grief!"** thought Miss Mallard. "This tells where the smugglers hide their **loot**. But does it mean over *this* bridge? And who is The Sneezer?"

At that moment, Miss Mallard

heard footsteps. The henchducks were standing overhead on the bridge!

"Did you check the windmill?" asked the first henchduck.

"She wasn't there," said the second henchduck. "What if we can't find her?"

"You know The Sneezer's orders," came the answer. "**He wants that book!** And he's sure that mallard has it! If we can't find her, we are to open the floodgates of the **dike** to keep our

operation from being discovered.

"So," he added, "let's go back to the car and keep looking. She couldn't have gotten far on her bicycle."

Miss Mallard kept very quiet until she heard a car drive away. Then she grabbed her bicycle and carried it up to the path. She looked all around. The hench-ducks were nowhere in sight. She spotted the windmill beyond the bridge and remembered Julia's secret message in the black book.

**"Eureka!"** thought Miss Mallard. "Julia said, 'Over the bridge the goods are stored.' **That must be it!** The smuggled goods are in the windmill."

# 5

## SOS

Miss Mallard went to the windmill and peeked through a window. Sure enough, the inside was filled with boxes and crates, overflowing with diamonds and paintings. Then she tried the door. The

henchducks had forgotten to lock it, and the place was deserted!

Miss Mallard ran inside the windmill and up the winding stairs to the top. She looked out a small window. Down below she could see the inn, and the innkeeper standing at the back door.

Nearby was the field that she had crossed, the cluster of trees, and the farmer busy changing a tire on his tractor.

Beside the field was a winding road and the henchducks in their

car. At the end of the road was a tiny town.

Miss Mallard narrowed her eyes. She could see a police station in the town. **Policeducks** were standing in front of the station. She got an idea.

**"I hope my plan works,"** she said.

Quickly, Miss Mallard took a mirror from her knitting bag. Holding it so it caught the sun, she began signaling the police station.

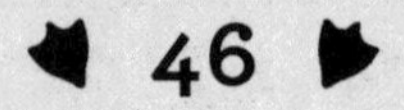

Her message in **Morse code** was for HELP:

Three short flashes.

Three long flashes.

Three more short flashes:

**SOS.**

Just then a policeduck saw the signal and pointed it out to the other officers. They all got on bicycles and began racing toward the windmill.

Miss Mallard kept on signaling:

**SOS. SOS. SOS.**

**Oh no!** The henchducks, the innkeeper, and the farmer also saw the signals! They came running toward Miss Mallard and her flashing lights.

The henchducks, the innkeeper, and the farmer arrived at the windmill before the police. Miss Mallard heard them open the door below and come up the stairs. **They were getting closer and closer.**

"What should I do now?" Miss Mallard worried.

# 6

# AAACHOO!

Miss Mallard waited for the right moment. Then, holding her knitting bag, she leaped from the window. With her free wing, she grabbed a **sail** of the windmill and rode swiftly to the ground.

Letting go of the sail, she took hold of a nearby rope and tied it to the wall. This made the sails stop turning, with one blocking the tiny window. That done, Miss Mallard shoved a stick through the handles of the door, locking it good and tight.

**"That will do it,"** said Miss Mallard. "That should keep each and every one locked up until the police get here."

When the police arrived, Miss Mallard told them about Julia, the

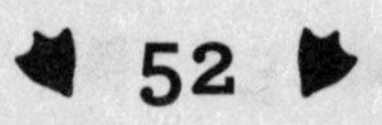

black book, and the smuggling ring.

"The leader of the ring—The Sneezer—is inside the windmill," said Miss Mallard.

She removed the **blunt** stick that fastened the door. Out came the henchducks, the farmer, and the innkeeper. The farmer sneezed loudly—**"AAACHOO!"** The policeducks grabbed him.

"Not him," said Miss Mallard. "He's *not* The Sneezer. He only has a cold. He probably just came here out of curiosity."

She removed a bottle from her knitting bag and started to spray perfume into the air.

**"No! No! Stop!"** yelled the innkeeper. "I'm **allergic**!"

Miss Mallard turned to the policeducks.

"There is your confession," she said. "The Sneezer is in fact the innkeeper. The inn is his hideout, and his hoard is in the windmill. These are his henchducks. He is allergic to flowers and perfume.

"I knew about his allergies," Miss Mallard continued, "when I saw the empty vases in the inn. I suspected him when he said *two* friends came for Julia. How could he have known that, when he claimed he was not there at the time? Two strikes against him!"

The police chief turned to the innkeeper. **"What have you done with Julia?"**

"She's back at the inn," the innkeeper grumbled. "I locked her in the attic."

"I'll go rescue her," said one of the policeducks.

The chief of police turned to Miss Mallard and said, "How can we ever thank you?"

"Easy," answered Miss Mallard. "Show me the quickest way back to my tour. They are a hearty group of cyclists, and I'm **anxious** to rejoin them."

"Not to worry," said the chief. "I'll **escort** you there myself."

**"What a thrill!"** exclaimed Miss Mallard.

# Word List

**aboard (a·BORED):** On a boat, train, or plane

**allergic (a·LURE·jik):** Having a reaction, such as sneezing or a rash, to a substance

**anxious (ANK·shus):** Nervous or worried something bad will happen

**blunt (BLUNT):** not sharp, having a thick edge

**clatter (KLA·tur):** A loud, sharp rattling noise

**cluster (KLUS·tir):** A small

group of things that are close together

**decode (dee·KODE):** To change from numbers, letters, or symbols into ordinary language

**dike (DIKE):** A high wall that is erected to prevent flooding

**escort (ess·KORT):** To go with a person to a place, sometimes in order to protect or guard him or her

**gloomy (GLUE·me):** Dim or dark, not sunny or bright

**hoard (HOARD):** A large number

of valuable items that are hidden or kept secret

**loot (LUTE):** Goods taken by stealing

**mastermind (MAS·tur·mined):** A clever person who plans a project in detail and makes sure it happens successfully

**Morse code (MORS KODE):** A system for sending messages in which letters or numbers are represented by dots and dashes or by short and long flashes of light or sounds

**promptly (PROMT·ly):** Exactly on time

**quaint (KWAYNT):** old-fashioned, cozy

**sail (SALE):** The part of a windmill that catches the wind

**smugglers (SMUG·lures):** People who take valuable goods into or out of a country secretly or illegally

**trench coats (TRENCH KOTES):** Long raincoats with belts and deep pockets

# Questions

1. What kind of secret code would you make up using both numbers and letters?
2. Why didn't secret agent Julia Pintail notify the police about the smugglers?
3. Who do you think was the mastermind of the smuggling ring?
4. After reading the code, where did you think the smuggled goods were hidden?
5. What other thing has a sail?

# Acknowledgments

My thanks and appreciation go to Jon Anderson, president and publisher of Simon & Schuster Children's Books, and his talented team: Karen Nagel, executive editor; Karin Paprocki, art director; Tiara Iandiorio, designer; Elizabeth Mims, managing editor; Bernadette Flinn, production manager; Tricia Lin, assistant editor; and Richard Ackoon, executive coordinator; for launching out into the world again these incredible new editions of my Miss Mallard Mystery books for today's young readers everywhere.